Minn and Jake's
Almost Terrible Summer

Minn and Jake's

Almost Terrible

Summer

Janet S. Wong
pictures by
Geneviève Côté

Frances Foster Books
Farrar, Straus and Giroux
New York

Text copyright © 2008 by Janet Wong
Pictures copyright © 2008 Geneviève Côté
Distributed in Canada by Douglas & McIntyre Ltd.
Printed in the United States of America
Designed by Jonathan Bartlett
First edition, 2008
10 9 8 7 6 5 4 3 2 1

www.fsgkidsbooks.com

Library of Congress Cataloging-in-Publication Data
Wong, Janet S.
    Minn and Jake's almost terrible summer / Janet Wong ; pictures
by Geneviève Côté.— 1st ed.
        p.   cm.
    Summary: Ten-year-old Jake's summer starts off badly, goes
downhill when his family visits Los Angeles, California, and his old
friends are too busy for him, then gets even worse after he
disagrees with Minn when her family joins his for a trip to
Disneyland.
    ISBN-13: 978-0-374-34977-6
    ISBN-10: 0-374-34977-0
    [1. Friendship—Fiction.   2. Summer—Fiction.   3. Family life—
California—Fiction.   4. Racially mixed people—Fiction.   5. Los
Angeles (Calif.)—Fiction.   6. Disneyland (Calif.)—Fiction.]   I. Côté,
Geneviève, ill.   II. Title.

PZ7.W842115 Min 2008
[Fic]—dc22

                                                        2007034416

JFic

To Frances Foster,
for your patience and support

Minn and Jake's
Almost Terrible Summer

1 / Summertime

A hundred years from now
when children go to school
all year round, every day,
old humpbacks with wrinkles
and black teeth will say,
Once upon a time,
when I was very young,
there was summer.
No school. You could sleep
until noon and play until midnight.
People ate sweet wet 'fruit'
that dangled down
from living ladders called 'trees.'
Summer was when everyone grew
two inches taller
and five brains wiser.
We had nine months of study,
and summertime to learn.

—

Jake wakes up and wonders:
is it July yet?

He remembers fireworks,
but he doesn't remember
if the fireworks were
Fourth of July fireworks

or Dodgers game fireworks
or New Year's Day fireworks—

or last year's fireworks.

Has July come and gone?

Every day the same,
no camps,
no lessons,
no school,
nothing to have to do:

Jake's Dream Summer.

Jake had begged for this,
plain old free time,
one big jumble
of sleeping
and eating
and playing video games.

Last summer
was too busy
with tennis camp
and science camp
and swimming lessons
and music lessons
and typing lessons,
camps and lessons,
lessons and camps,
one week after the next.

Jake had begged for nothing to do

because Jake had not expected
his brother Soup bouncing
and bouncing
and bouncing on the bed
every single morning
at six o'clock.

Jake had not expected
to be stuffed,
force-fed five pounds of food each day
by his grandmother,
whose summer project
is to make him grow.

Jake had not expected
that his mother
would plop down on the couch next to him
and try to learn to play video games,
blabbing,
Isn't this too violent?
Do we keep on shooting?
Is he bleeding blue*?*

Jake had begged—for *this*?

These days of nothing to do
are moving so achingly s-l-o-w-l-y.

Yesterday seems a full week ago.

At the same time, though,
the weeks seem to be flying by:
vacation will be over in a month!

Jake is wondering
if he has wasted his summer.

⸺

Jake is worrying
about the first day of school.

When other kids will brag about trips
to Yosemite
and Mount Rushmore
and Niagara Falls
and the Grand Canyon,
Mexico, Canada,
Europe, Asia, Africa, and Australia—

Jake will have nothing to say.

Jake is wishing he had agreed to go
to chess camp, math camp,
boot camp, any camp.
Jake makes a note in his notebook:
Is there camp in Antarctica?

Jake is wishing
his family were rich.

Jake is wishing
his family went on adventures.

Jake is wishing
he had stayed
home
in Santa Brunella,
and while his father worked
in the city,
Jake could've spent busy days
with his friend Minn,
catching lizards
and digging tunnels for worms.

Jake doesn't even like catching lizards
and digging tunnels for worms,
but Jake is beginning to feel
like a rotten plum
because he hasn't been a friend
to Minn all summer.

He called her twice
to answer the letters
she sent him every week,
but he didn't leave much of a message
either time.

It's been almost two weeks
since the last letter,
so maybe Minn has given up.

Which would be the right thing
for her to do.

Because who ever heard
of such opposites being friends, anyway—

should a tall lizard-catching girl
and a short city boy be best friends?

2 / The Pits

Jake had thought
it would be fun coming back home
to Los Angeles
to play with his old friends.

Jake was wrong.

The worst part of moving
is coming back to visit.
You come back
to the old neighborhood
and everyone asks you,
again and again,
So, how is it there? You like it?

YOU: It's OK.

THEM: New friends?

YOU: One friend.

THEM: ONE friend?
One friend?
Only one friend?

You hate the way
people ask the same question
over and over
when they don't get the answer they want.

So you let them win:
you change the answer.

YOU: A lot of friends, I guess,
but only one really good friend.
Really, really, really good friend.

THEM: What kind of sports does he do?

Maybe you shouldn't have changed the answer.
Maybe you should've let them ask
the same "one friend" question
until they got thirsty for a soda pop.

YOU: She doesn't do any sports, really. She—

THEM: She?

YOU: Yeah, she—she catches lizards.

THEM: Lizards! Lizards?
Jake, she whats? SHE?

Now the trouble really starts.
They can't believe
you have only one friend,
but that's nothing
compared to the fact that it's a girl.
She's a girl. A girl?
And this girl touches lizards?
Catches them!

They ask you to say her name over and over:
Men? A girl named Men?

You spell the name.
You only have one friend—
a girl named Minn
(short for Minnie, you lie)—
who catches lizards.
They look at you
and then they look away.
You know what they're thinking:
If you have become strange
and unpopular,
then being friends with you
would make them strange
and unpopular, too.

THEM: She's not your girlfriend, is she?

YOU: No, NO! She's TALL!
I wouldn't even be able to kiss her
unless I was standing on a ladder!
(Oh, no, why did you say that?!)
You change the subject, quickly.
Want to go to the movies around four o'clock?

You're hoping
they'll come to the movies
and invite you to have dinner,
play video games, sleep over—
just like you used to do all the time—
but, sorry.

They have soccer practice.
Grandparents are in town.
Little sister is sick.

Or they look at their moms
and the moms say sorry.
The moms pat your head.
Your best friends.
They used to be your best friends.
Now they can't even find time for a movie.

All summer long Jake has been trading calls
with friends who are too busy to play.

Half the summer has already been swallowed up
like a handful of cherries—

and Jake is left
with nothing but the pits.

3 / The Edeska All-You-Can't-Eat Buffet

Mogo-mogo-MAANI-mogo!
Jake's grandmother, his *halmoni*,
herds Jake toward the fried noodles.
Jake doesn't speak Korean,
but he understands this,
because Halmoni says it ten times a day:
Mogo-mogo-MAANI-mogo!
Eat-eat-eat! LOTS!

Halmoni weighs only 103 pounds,
but she eats triple
what Jake and his mother combined
can just barely force themselves to swallow.

They make too much money off you,
Halmoni tells her daughter.

Jake's mother frowns at Halmoni.
The frown bounces from Halmoni to Jake.
Ouch!
Jake's stomach hurts.
And his chest.
And his back.
His eyebrows, even.
Jake is beginning to sweat and shake.

Halmoni goes back
to fill her plate an eighth time,
this time

with her favorite spicy tuna sushi.
Soup heads straight to the dessert line.
He fills his ninth plate
with apple sponge cake,
chocolate chunk cheesecake,
a blueberry crepe,
and three slices of watermelon.
Halmoni and Soup
waddle back to the table.

This is not an eating contest.
Better not get sick, Soup!
But just as Jake says it,
he feels an urge to regurgitate
his tiny plate of fried noodles.

Jake pushes Soup out of their booth
and bolts for the bathroom.
He is almost at the bathroom door—

almost.

Jake's mother pushes him
into the ladies' room
to finish the lava flow.
She rushes outside
to wipe up the mess.

Jake comes out of the toilet stall
with his pukey shirt.
Two girls point, holding their noses.

Jake walks out the bathroom door
and his mother pushes him in again,
lifting his shirt carefully up
over the back of his head.
She rinses it and wrings it out,
but the shirt is still smelly.
And soaking wet.

Here, wear this, Jake's mother says,
pulling her pink overshirt off
and adjusting her flowery tank top.

Pink? Flower buttons?
Jake pushes the shirt away
and starts walking out the door
when his mother pinches his ear,
yanking him back.
She shoves his arms into the pink shirt
and Jake walks out—

just as Haylee Hirata walks in.
Perfect Haylee Hirata,
the girl Jake had a crush on
in kindergarten,
and first grade,
not second grade
(when her front teeth were missing) but
third grade
and fourth grade, too. Haylee Hirata,
the love he left behind last year
when he moved to Santa Brunella—

the love he would have left behind,
if he had ever gotten up the nerve
to do more than hit her in dodgeball.

Jake?

Haylee?

Jake, isn't this the girls' bathroom?

Back at the table,
Jake's jacket pocket rings.
Soup answers Jake's cell phone.
Minn? Minn!

Soup stands on his seat and yells,
Jake, it's Minn!

Then Soup shouts into the phone,
loudly enough for the whole restaurant to hear,
Minn, Jake can't talk right now
because he puked
and he just came out of the girls' bathroom
with Mommy's pink shirt on—
and he's busy talking to his girlfriend Haylee—

Girlfriend? Minn asks. *Girlfriend?*
Who?

Haylee Hirata. She's so pretty, Minn!
Prettier than your friend Sabina.

And short like Jake.
Perfect to be his girlfriend! Soup giggles.
Except, wait!
Minn, isn't Jake's girlfriend
YOU?

4 / Boyfriend and Girlfriend

MINN: Hello? (Are you OK?)

JAKE: I'm miserable. Miserable!
(Can you imagine, puking all over the place?)

MINN: Puked all over the place, huh?
(You were in the girls' bathroom?)

JAKE: Five steps from the bathroom door.

MINN: In front of . . . your girlfriend?
(Is she really your girlfriend?)

JAKE: (Just a girl from my old school.)
Haylee.

MINN: Yup. (Your mom's shirt?)

JAKE: (Can you believe my mom?)
She put the stupid pink shirt on me,
she buttoned the buttons (daisy buttons!),
she wiped my chin like a baby. PINK!
(I can't even stand to think about it now.)

MINN: Call me later, then.
I need to tell you about my news—
(Will you be home tomorrow?)

JAKE: Call me tomorrow.
I'll be home. Same as every day.

MINN: We need to talk!
(I have news for you!)

JAKE: OK, I'll call you
later. Soon. I promise!

When you talk with a good friend,
half the conversation is in parentheses.
You know what your friend is thinking.
When you talk with a stranger,
it's like homework.
Complete sentences.
Questions to get answers.

With a true best friend,
the questions are understood,
the answers are automatic,
and knowing you've ruined your friend's day
with your bad news
somehow makes it easier to bear.

Jake has indeed ruined Minn's day.

She had wanted to tell him
that her parents surprised her this morning
by giving her an early birthday present:
a trip to Los Angeles.
Minn's mother needs to work in Los Angeles
and her father found cheap plane tickets

so they could join her.
They'll be there tomorrow night!

Minn wanted so badly to tell,
but Jake didn't seem to want to hear.

Anyway, you cannot tell someone this kind of news
when they are still in shock
over puking
and being forced to wear a pink shirt.

And Minn has seen that pink shirt
on Jake's mom.
It has perky daisy buttons,
and dainty white lace around the collar.
Poor dainty Jake.

—

Haylee Hirata:
Why did Jake never talk about her before?
Small, just like him. Pretty.
Undoubtedly dainty.
Minn wonders,
Is she the kind that wears fingernail polish
and glitter lip gloss, like Sabina?

Minn wonders if Jake likes Sabina.
How else would Soup know who Sabina was?
How would Soup know that Sabina was pretty,
if Jake hadn't said anything?

Jake and Sabina did spend a lot of time
alone
talking with each other,
after Jake became a hero
on Valentine's Day,
calling 9-1-1
to fish Minn out of the Gulch.

Sabina even hugged him!
And she had no excuse for hugging him.
Minn should've been the only one
doing the hugging,
since she was the one Jake rescued.
Minn replays the scene in her mind,
like a video:
The Hug. The HUG. *Sabina's* H-U-G.
And Jake almost kind-of hugged back!

Minn looks at her fingernails.
Her short, chipped fingernails,
caked with dirt.
She looks at her lips in the mirror.
Her dry, plain lips.

Jake hasn't answered any of her letters.
Is it because of her dry, plain lips?

Would Jake like her better
if she wore fingernail polish
and lip gloss?

And if he liked her better that way,
would she still like him?

—

Minn runs outside
and jumps up into a tree,
using her leather belt
to climb it like a pro.
Sitting in the oak tree,
she watches squirrels chase each other
and chitter-chatter around her.
Minn pulls her notebook out of her pocket
and draws three squirrels.

She writes:

Thursday, July 17, 3:10 p.m.:

Weather:
too hot

Description of squirrels:
Big Bushy Light Gray one (BB)
with part of her very bushy tail bitten off,
likes to pause a lot,
chases Medium-sized Dark Gray one (MD),
then almost falls off a branch and gives up

seems BB wants MD for a boyfriend
(but probably just wants to play)

MD runs away

MD does not want BB for a girlfriend

MD then starts chasing
Tiny Shiny Brownish Gray one (TS)

TS likes being chased
(what a tease!)

Minn pauses. She watches the hawks. She finishes:

Poor lonely clumsy big BB.

5 / Wake Up, Jake!

Every morning
Jake wakes up at six o'clock
from Soup bouncing on his bed,
on his pillows,
on his head,
and the smells of
Halmoni's huge breakfast buffet
greet him.

Halmoni doesn't seem to understand
that fried fish is not good breakfast food.

Kimchi cabbage is even worse.

But there's plenty to choose from:
watermelon and pineapple,
boiled eggs and bacon,
rice and fried noodles,
kalbi beef and fish—

enough food for ten people!

After breakfast,
Halmoni, Soup, and Jake's mother
go to visit Halmoni's doctors.

And Jake goes back to sleep.

The diabetes doctor says
Halmoni's diabetes is so serious,
sooner or later, if she doesn't change,
they will need to cut off her foot.

The vein doctor says
they can try Roto-Rooter surgery
on the veins in Halmoni's leg
to fix her problem.
If the Roto-Rooter works,
they won't have to cut her foot off.

Jake likes the vein doctor
better than the diabetes doctor.

Jake does not like thinking
about Halmoni
clomping around with one foot.

This morning
Jake cannot fall back asleep.
He is staring at the ceiling,
looking at the floaters
in his eyes,
following the gray amoebas
up, down, and across.

Back and forth,
the amoeba-floaters hypnotize Jake.

He starts to dream.
The dream seems like a movie scene:

Jake is at a restaurant,
but this restaurant doesn't serve food.
It serves electronics.

JAKE: I'll have a cell phone, please.

The waiters are robots,
thin, elegant, flying machines,
the most beautiful robots Jake has seen.
Jake's robot opens her front panel
to reveal phones, arranged like ribs.
She asks which one he'd like.
She delivers the question silently,
telepathically, on brain waves.
Jake answers back
by scratching his head.
A new cell phone, lighter than air,
appears in his hand.

It auto-dials Haylee's number.

JAKE: Hello, is Haylee there?

Minn answers. Minn?!

MINN: Jake, is that you?
Who are you calling?
This is Minn!
This Haylee-Haylee stuff

is really bugging me.
If I hear Haylee's name one more time,
I'm going to scream!
I thought I was your best friend!
Don't you care about me anymore?
Why don't you write?
Don't you want to hear my news?

Jake wakes up.
He checks his cell phone
to make sure that he didn't call Haylee.

He checks again
to make sure that he didn't call Minn.

What a nightmare!

Jake runs to the pantry
and grabs a bag of potato chips
and a handful of cookies
for his mid-morning snack.

Even though Halmoni feeds him constantly,
she never gives him what he wants to eat.
Jake is starving for potato chips and cookies.

One bite, and the key turns in the lock.
Jake stuffs three cookies in his mouth at once,
stuffs another three in his pockets,
and hides the potato chips
under the pillow on the couch.

Soup bounds in
and jumps on the pillow. *Crunch!*

What's that noise?
Jake, let's go ask Misha to play!

Jake agrees to walk Soup
to Misha's house.
When they get there,
Jake sits on the front lawn.
You play. I'll stay here and take a nap.

Misha answers the door.
He squeals
when he sees Soup.
We can play with water guns
or build a new Lego garage or—
anything you want, Soup!

Anything you want—
Jake wishes he were five years old again,
back when friendship was easy.

Jake sits on the front lawn
and pulls his cell phone
out of his pocket.
One bar of signal.
No messages.
He remembers his dream about Minn.
He also remembers something about news.
Was that in his dream,

or in his conversation?
Did Minn say something about news?

Jake puts his phone back in his pocket
and settles flat on the grass,
his eyes closed.
The sun on his face feels good,
the soft grass on his legs.

He wakes up a half hour later.
The grass is tickling his legs.
Crawling on his legs.
Biting.
Grass, crawling and biting?
Suddenly, Jake sees:
hundreds of ants are swarming
up his legs
and disappearing in his pants,
invading his pockets.

The cookies!

Jake jumps up. He scratches
and swats at himself.
He turns his pockets inside out.
No good: the ants are in his underwear.
He is dancing a crazy dance
with both his hands
inside his pants
just when a blue Mercedes
pulls in front of the driveway to drop off
Haylee's little brother Jeremy.

Haylee is sitting in the front seat.
Haylee, Haylee, Haylee!

Jake pulls his hands out of his pants.
Now the ants are traveling up his shirt.
Jake reaches for his armpits.

Hose him down! Grab the hose!
Take your shirt off!
Misha's mom shouts.
Jake takes off his shirt.
Misha grabs the hose.
Jeremy turns the water on, full-blast.
Soup grabs Jake
by the top of his boxer shorts.
Misha sprays him in the face.

Haylee's car pauses in the street.
Haylee puts the window down
and calls Jeremy over.
She says something to Jeremy,
and he makes high-pitched whale noises
while Haylee laughs
so loudly
she cackles like a chicken,
then snorts—
yes, snorts like a pig!
Beautiful, graceful—
yes, dainty, even—
Haylee Hirata:
Cackling like a chicken?
Snorting like a pig?

Jake stares in disbelief
as the car speeds off,
Haylee's barnyard laughter
fouling the air
around him.

6 / Instant Brown

When they get home from Misha's,
Soup asks,
Jake, what's a beluga whale?

A funny-looking oddball white whale,
Jake answers.

Soup starts laughing so hard
he cannot breathe,
and Jake needs to tickle the why
out of Soup,
who almost chokes
on a chunk of watermelon
when he says,
Haylee told Jeremy
your chest is whiter
than a beluga whale!

Jake rushes into the bathroom.
He lifts his shirt up.
Haylee's right: he's whiter
than a beluga whale.
When Jake gets tanned,
he doesn't look good and brown.
He looks kind of pink and raw.
Jake wishes he had more Korean in him.
Just then, he remembers
the "Instant Brown" tanning lotion
he tipped over yesterday

while reaching for the toilet paper
under the sink.

Instant Brown:
Jake hopes it works.
He tries a little patch.
Funny, it has no color.
Jake puts more on, a handful.
He slaps it all over.
Instant brown? Still white.
He slathers it on his chest.
He runs fingers full of it
up his legs and across his feet.

Jake prays.
Dear God, if You exist:
please-please-please do not let
Haylee Hirata
see my white chest and legs again,
and please make this Instant Brown stuff
turn me really, really, brown.
Thank you. Amen.

Sitting on the toilet,
Jake reads the label
on the bottle of Instant Brown:
Goes on white, but reacts
with your own body oils
to give you a deep, dark tan
overnight!

Suddenly Jake remembers: MINN!
Why does he keep forgetting
to call her?

Jake takes his cell phone out
and calls her then and there.
You're coming to town—
tonight?!

Minn and Jake decide
they should all meet at Uncle Joon's.
Jake's uncle has a new restaurant
in Santa Monica:
Old Village Barbecue, on Ocean Park.
Tonight is the Grand Opening.

Minn says she loves barbecue.
Jake knows she's thinking
of Texas barbecue
or Memphis barbecue,
finger-licking sticky sauce on ribs.

Korean barbecue is totally different.
What will Minn think
of smelly kimchi
and little dried fishes,
and garlic, garlic in everything?

Minn! Minn! Soup says.
He runs to Minn and gives her a python-hug.
Minn, did you bring me a lizard?

No, no lizards, Minn says.

No lizards? That's OK.
Because . . .
I have lizards for you!
Soup reaches into his backpack
and pulls out a jar of tiny gray lizards
that he caught with Misha
that afternoon.

Minn peers into the jar.
Poor things, you look sick.
Soup, how long have they been in there?
What have you been feeding them?

Soup describes their lunch
of candy bar bits
and soda.

Minn protests.
No, no! Oh, no!
You need to let them go!

Soup starts to unscrew the lid
of the peanut butter jar.
Not now. Not here! Jake hisses.
We'll say when.

You'll say when, Soup says.

Jake says,
Put the lizards back in your backpack.
Minn, come and meet everyone.
Jake walks to the back of the restaurant,
near the kitchen door. Minn follows,
with Soup holding her hand.
These are our cousins Colin and Shiree.

Halmoni comes through the kitchen door,
holding a tray full of small panchan dishes.

And that's our grandmother, our halmoni.

That's your grandmother? Minn whispers.
Your grandmother is Asian?

That's our Korean grandmother, Jake says.
We also had a German grandmother,
but she died before I was born.

Mogo-mogo-MAANI-mogo! Halmoni says.

Uncle Joon introduces himself
but excuses himself just as quickly,
rushing back to the kitchen.

Minn looks bewildered
by the dozen little dishes of food.
She picks up the little plate of kimchi
and empties it on her plate.

Soup laughs.
You don't eat the whole thing by yourself!
Everybody shares everything on the table.
Here comes the kalbi beef!

The waitress puts a plate of meat
in front of Minn—
raw meat swimming in a shallow puddle of blood.
This is for me? Minn asks.
She hopes the answer is no.

No, but you can cook it,
Soup says, pointing at the grill in front of Minn.
The waitress turns the gas on.
She puts the slabs of meat on the grill,
with tongs placed in front of Minn.

I cook it? Minn asks.

Girls always cook it, Soup says.
Mom or Shiree or Halmoni.
Never dads or boys.

Shiree quickly grabs the tongs
and switches places with Minn.

Minn is now sitting at the end of the table
across from Jake,
away from the sizzling kalbi.

She whispers,
You didn't tell me you were Asian!

Jake whispers back,
Did you ever tell me that you're white?

Jake explains his hapa heritage.
Hapa = slang for half-white, half-Asian.
His mother is half-Korean, half-Norwegian.
His father is half-German, half-French.

Minn points out that Jake is not hapa, then,
but three-quarters white,
and only one-quarter Asian.

OK, then, Jake says. *Quarpa. I'm quarpa.*
Jake likes the sound of *quarpa.*
It sounds like something with superpowers.

*Wish you'd told me before
that you were Korean,* Minn says.
You didn't need to surprise me with it.

And why should I have told you?

Because it's who you are, Jake.

Jake cannot believe his ears.
How can his friend Minn,
who is so smart in school,
seem so stupid now?
*But you don't care
that I never told you
I'm part Norwegian
and part French and part German!*

And did I ever tell you
that I like taking bubble baths
and playing Halo 2 until midnight?
Did I?

Minn cannot believe her ears.
You like taking bubble baths?
What kind of a boy takes bubble baths?

Jake lashes back.
Have you ever taken a bubble bath
in your whole life?
What kind of a girl
doesn't like bubble baths?!

They spend the rest of the meal in silence,
eating kimchi, gulping water,
and fanning their flaming tongues.

7 / Venice Beach

The next morning Jake is awakened
by Soup shrieking,
Oh, no! You have a disease!
You have a skin disease!
Mommy, hurry!
Is he contagious?

Jake's arms and legs are orange-brown—
and striped like a tiger.

Soup pushes Jake's T-shirt up.
Jake's chest is mottled,
dappled with brown spots
and large splotches—
all on a creamy white background.
He looks like a springer spaniel,
or an Appaloosa—
or a boy who doesn't know how to use
Instant Brown.

Jake's mother laughs.
You found my old bottle
of Instant Brown tanning lotion, did you?
Don't worry. If you scrub hard, it'll come off—
in about a week.

But Jake and Soup are taking Minn
to Venice Beach today!

When Minn arrives, one look at his skin
sends her howling.

How can you stay mad
at a friend who looks like a spotted hyena—
even when he does say
obnoxious things all the time?

You might know
how to find your way around in the wild,
Jake brags, *but I know my way around here.*
Don't laugh. You need to watch out.
It can be kind of wild,
especially with the crowds at Venice Beach.
Watch out for pickpockets.
You need street smarts, Minn,
and no offense, but—

Watching out for pickpockets isn't hard.
When you walk up and down Venice Beach,
watching is the whole point: people-watching.
You walk up and down the boardwalk,
and you look at the oily bodybuilders
and their bulging muscles,
girls with spiky green hair
and earrings in their lips
and noses
and eyebrows,
Rollerblading guitar players,
the Golden Man who stands like a statue
until you put money in his box,
chainsaw jugglers,

fire-eaters, tattoo artists,
fortune tellers, magicians.

Hey, everybody! Soup shouts.
Look! Ice cream!

A red-faced,
red-haired man
in a striped red shirt shouts,
*Welcome
to the Second Annual
Frojjen Moudde
Ice Cream Eating Contest!*

*Our competitors today
will try to beat last year's record
of 32 ice cream cones in ten minutes,
set by our defending champion,
Wanda the Wonder Eater!*

Kids, don't try this at home!

*We don't want you
to freeze your mouths
and bite your tongues off
and choke and die
and sue us for millions of dollars,
now do we?*

Yes-we-DO! Soup shouts.
Can I be in the contest?

A skinny woman on Rollerblades,
her arms and legs covered with tattoos, shouts,
Hey, this kid wants to be in the contest!

The red man explains
how he's hoping to make this contest
an official event next year.

The International Federation of Competitive Eating,
the IFOCE, says that no one
under the age of eighteen
can compete—

The crowd boos.
The skinny woman starts a chant.
The crowd joins in:
Let him eat!
Let him compete!

Rules are rules, the red man tells the crowd.

The skinny woman skates away.
The crowd starts to break up and leave.
A woman dressed in a bright yellow
Frojjen Moudde suit
whispers into the red man's ear.

Wait a minute, everybody!
Come on up, son!
Even though you can't officially compete,
we're going to let you eat as much
Frojjen Moudde ice cream as you want—

while our professional eaters
are doing their jobs!

The three competitors are introduced.
Gerry the UPS Man
looks like a summer version of Santa Claus.
He raises his arms high in the air
when he is introduced,
stands on tiptoes like a ballerina,
and bows. The crowd hoots and cheers.

The next competitor is Muumuu LuLu,
a woman with a tiny pretty face
swallowed up in folds of fat.
Minn wonders how Muumuu Lulu
can open her tiny mouth wide enough
to fit gallons of ice cream.
Clearly, though, Muumuu LuLu
has somehow managed
in the past
to do her fair share of eating.

The last competitor
is Wanda the Wonder Eater,
a quiet and skinny Asian woman.
The crowd claps politely for Wanda,
but Wanda does not seem to hear them.
She must be in a trance, meditating on the cones.

She's gonna lose, Minn says.
She's so skinny.

My halmoni is skinny, Jake says,
and you have no idea how much she eats.
Besides, didn't Wanda win last year?

Soup then introduces himself
as *Soup the Super Eater!*
The crowd erupts
with cheers and whistles
when he does a mini Gerry-Ballerina twirl.

Are you ready?

YES! the crowd shouts.

Gerry the Hippo Ballerina
jumps out to an early lead.
At the five-minute mark,
he is ahead with 20 cones.
His "bite-chew-swallow" technique
looks hard to beat—
but his nose is running
and his face is turning purple.

Muumuu LuLu's small mouth
does not seem to be a problem.
She is in second place.
Her eyes are watering, though,
and she keeps shivering,
which makes her look
like she's trying to do the hula
sitting down.

Both Gerry and LuLu have nearly quit
while Wanda is catching up,
slow and steady,
eating with no breaks,
no heavy breathing,
no lip-slapping,
no shivers or sighs.
At the five-minute mark,
Wanda has only 16 cones,
but she shows no signs of slowing down.

Jake is glad that Soup is not competing.
Soup is an embarrassment:
he is licking his ice cream cones,
biting, chewing,
standing up,
sitting down,
standing up, walking around,
licking, slurping,
biting some more,
and even occasionally shoving a whole scoop
in his mouth with his fingers.

At the five-minute mark,
he has eaten only 10 cones.

At the eight-minute mark, though,
while Gerry and LuLu have practically quit,
Soup is still eating strong.

He is almost keeping pace with Wanda
cone-for-cone,

a mini-clone
of The Eating Machine herself.

The crowd has tripled in size.
A teenage girl with purple hair
and a purple bikini yells,
Go Super-boy!

A man selling sunglasses shouts,
Watch that kid!
Can you believe it?
That kid can eat!

Minn starts chanting,
Soup! Soup! Soup! Soup!
The crowd joins in.
When the buzzer sounds,
Jake thrusts his arms up in victory.
That's my brother! Soup!
That's my brother! YESSSS!

No one cares that Wanda the Wonder Eater
has broken her record with 33 cones
in ten minutes.

All eyes are on the frozen smile
of Soup the Super Eater,
unofficially in fourth and last place,
but pound-for-pound
the undisputed winner:

Gerry the UPS Man: 28 ice cream cones
Muumuu LuLu: 26 ice cream cones
Wanda the Wonder Eater: 33 ice cream cones
Soup the Super Eater: 23 ice cream cones

Great job, Soup! Minn says,
covering Soup's frozen face
with kisses.

I have a stomachache, Soup says.
He runs to the bathroom tent,
holding his stomach.
Jake runs after him.

Five minutes pass.
You didn't fall in the hole, did you?
Jake says to the Porta-Potty door.
Soup groans.
Another five minutes later,
Soup comes out smiling.

OK now? Jake asks.

Soup gives the thumbs-up sign.

Minn says, *I'm hungry
from watching all that eating.
Who wants a hot dog?*

Soup raises his hand
and jumps up and down, shouting,
I do! I do! And can I have a churro, too?

8 / Halmoni's Spending Sprees

Halmoni is not rich,
but she loves to spend money
on Jake and Soup,
which Jake and Soup love—
except that their parents always scold them
for letting Halmoni buy too much.

Halmoni is itching to buy something today,
and with Jake's mother gone
to visit her friends,
and Minn spending the rest of the day
with her father,
and Soup's eating feat to celebrate,
it's the perfect time to do it.

Halmoni, Jake, and Soup plan their day.
First stop: GameStop.

Soup says,
Misha gave me a GameStop card yesterday.
Mommy has it in her purse.
I'll tell her to bring it to me.
Let's call her, Jake!

No, no! Jake says.
You can't tell Mom about any of this!

Halmoni nods vigorously,
her eyes darting around like a criminal.

She and Jake exchange sly glances
and hand signals.

Jake wants to look at the used games.
Not because
Jake wants to buy used games,
but because
he wants to know what's available
and how much things cost,
so he can trade his used games.

Barter can be big business.
Last summer
Jake traded a Sony PSP game
for a brand-new bike.

It went like this:

1. Jake traded
a Sony PSP game (Lumines)
to Mariela
for an *Anchorman* DVD;

2. Jake then traded
Anchorman
to his cousin Colin
for a huge tae kwon do trophy
that Colin was using as a hat rack;

3. Next Jake traded
the tae kwon do trophy
to Jeremy (Haylee Hirata's brother)

for an autographed baseball
that Jeremy's grandfather had given him.
Jeremy made the trade
because he had no idea
who the baseball player was,
and he was sick of
hearing his parents bragging
about Haylee's tae kwon do trophies;

4. Finally Jake traded
the Pete Rose autographed baseball
to Jake's father's best friend
and got a brand new Diamondback mountain bike,
with a free water bottle thrown in.

So Jake is doing research at GameStop,
checking out the competition:

> Zero copies of Star Wars Battlefront II.
> Zero copies of Halo.
> Zero copies of Halo 2.

This would make it a very easy sell
or trade (for Jake),
if he were willing
to part with any of those games.
But he's not.
And unfortunately
there are three copies of Gladius
and six copies of Sneakers,
the two games
that Jake was hoping to trade this week.

Too much supply.

Next stop: Best Buy.
The games that Jake and Soup want
aren't any cheaper there
than they were (new) at GameStop.

But Jake's mother
will raise her eyebrows
over a GameStop bag.

And she won't care much
about a Best Buy bag—
especially
if Jake also happens to buy blank CDs.

Jake's mother doesn't need to know
that in addition to blank CDs—
they bought three video games, too.

Looking at all the video games,
it hits Jake:
somebody came up with the ideas
for each of these video games.
People: why not him?

An idea for a video game
pops into Jake's head,
and he scribbles it quickly
in the little notebook he keeps in his pocket,
afraid that the idea will disappear.

This might be the game
that turns Jake
from a sitting-on-the-couch amateur gamer
into a professional video game developer,

from a regular kid
into—a millionaire!

Jake writes:

Stuff It!

Object of game:
stuff your face with the most food

Setting: an eating contest

Characters:
a multi-player first-person eating game;
look at a line-up of eaters
and choose who you want to be

Special effects:
an aroma-maker console attachment
shoots out puffs of food smells
(chocolate, pizza, peaches, burgers, popcorn)

Levels:
advance to a different level
with each ten pounds of food you eat

Level One:
something easy to eat
(easy to grab with the controls),
such as hamburgers

Level Two:
something harder to eat
(harder to grab with the controls
and harder to eat in real life),
such as broccoli

Level Three:
something really hard to eat,
like worms

When you eat (grab/shoot/whatever)
a pound of food, you earn points.

Bacteria are trying to sneak into your food.
You need to shoot them down.
    Salmonella = 5 points
    E. coli = 10 points

When you accidentally eat contaminated food,
you vomit (and lose points and eventually can
die).

Maybe Soup isn't so bad, after all,
Jake is thinking.

If Soup hadn't entered the eating contest,
Jake never would have come up with this idea,
and then Jake wouldn't become
a millionaire (next year) at age eleven.

Jake is waiting for Soup and Halmoni
to come back from the bathroom.
He is sitting on the edge
of the mall's large reflecting pool,
estimating the coins at the bottom,
when he starts wondering
how he will spend his first million.

Jake is scribbling:

> Aston Martin (a James Bond car)?
> boat?
> private airpla

when Soup ambushes him from behind,
causing Jake's notebook
to go flying—

straight into the water!

Soup! Jake screams.

But before Jake can say *YOU STUPID ID*—
Soup jumps in after the notebook,
grabs it, holds it high in the air,
and shouts,
Soup to the rescue!

9 / The Happiest Place on Earth

The next day, 10:15 a.m.:
Minn's father gets in line
for tickets at Disneyland.
Halmoni fights
over who gets to pay.
She stuffs three
one hundred dollar bills
in his pocket.

10:20 a.m.: Minn's father finds the bills
and passes them
behind his back
to Minn's mother,
who stuffs them
in Halmoni's huge overstuffed purse
when she is not looking.

10:30 a.m.: Soup wants to go
on Small World first
and Teacups next.
Jake wants to go
on Indiana Jones.
Minn wants to go
on the Pirates of the Caribbean ride.
Minn's father mentions
that the Haunted Mansion,
his favorite ride ever since
his own summer
between fifth and sixth grade,

thirty years ago,
will have a shorter line.
Minn's mother wants to go
to the California Adventure side
and ride Soarin' Over California.
They argue.

10:40 a.m.: They are still arguing.
Minn grimaces.

10:45 a.m.: Minn's mother says,
Stop making that face.
We're not arguing, honey—
aren't we allowed to TALK?

Jake suggests that they split up.
You three go your way.
Soup and Halmoni can go
to Small World,
and I'll go on Indiana Jones.
We'll meet up at one o'clock.

Minn mutters,
And why
did we bother coming here
together?

Jake points out
they should've decided this in the car.
And why
didn't we decide this in the car?

Haunted Mansion

Small World

Teacups

Pirates

Indiana Jones

You Are Here

Soarin'

N
W   E
S

Was somebody
too busy reading her REPTILE book?

11:15 a.m.: They get in line
at Pirates. Halmoni was walking
like a tortoise today,
stopping every hundred feet
to pound her aching leg.
It took half an hour
to walk from the park entrance
to Pirates of the Caribbean.

Jake has convinced Soup
that he should save the best for last.

Going on Pirates first
is like spinach salad at dinner,

and going on Indiana Jones next
is like spaghetti and meatballs
(a much better part of the meal),

and going on Small World and Teacups
at the very end
is just like a double dessert:
ice cream and pie!

—

11:45 a.m.: Pirates of the Caribbean
has one of the longest
and slowest-moving lines

of any ride in the whole park.
The line is moving
about six inches a minute.

This would not be bad
if the line were six feet long,
but the thick clumpy line
(three or four children across at some points)
is winding around the chain barriers,
up and down and side to side
for at least six hundred feet,
as far as the eye can see.

If people were coins
at the bottom of a fountain,
Jake figures there would be at least
2,000 copper pennies,
500 nickels,
and 300 quarters
in front of him.

Noon: Three boys
push their way past.
Our mom is up there,
the biggest boy says.
Jake follows them with his eyes.
They stop about four rows up,
tapping the shoulder
of the woman in front of them.
They are acting friendly
toward her,
as if she is their mother.

But she is not acting friendly
toward them.
They do not look like family.
Jake points this out to Minn.

Minn snaps,
You and Soup
don't look exactly like Halmoni, either,
do you?

Just as they are about to turn a corner
into a different waiting room,
Soup spies a family
five or six rows over,
near the beginning of the line,
that looks like the Hirata family.
That's Jeremy! And Haylee!
Soup says, pointing.

Where? Minn says,
straining to see.

Jake says,
Why do you want to see?

Minn answers,
I'm curious.
I'm curious to see
what your GIRLFRIEND looks like.

It's not them, Jake says.

You didn't even look! Minn says.

Yes, I did, Jake lies.

Minn hisses,
You didn't turn your head!
You liar!

12:15 p.m.: Minn and Jake
are no longer talking.
They're almost
at the front of the line.
A large group of Fastpass people
whiz by, legally cutting
in front
of the poor
Fastpass-less masses.

Minn says, *We're so stupid.*
We should've gotten Fastpasses
for the Haunted Mansion
before getting in line here.

No one says a thing,
because they all know she is right.

The next half hour is lost
in time,
or pirate-space,
or Disney-reality.
Or maybe
that half hour didn't happen at all?

Suddenly Jake looks at his watch
and it is 12:54.

12:55 p.m.: The front of the line!

Jake does the calculations:
they waited one hour and forty minutes
for the Pirates ride,
which will last about fifteen minutes,
which means
they have waited almost seven minutes
for each one minute
of the ride.

12:56 p.m.: Soup has to go
to the bathroom.
He is clutching his pants and dancing.
Halmoni whispers something to Soup
and he nods.

Their boat arrives.
Jake starts moving toward it,
but the Disney worker holds him back,
motioning toward a pale blond girl
sitting in a wheelchair
in the special lane for disabled people.

Three giggling girls shuffle in,
behind the chair.

They're with me,
the wheelchair girl says.

Two of the giggling girls
have blond hair, too.
They could be sisters.
The third giggling girl has black hair.
She is Asian.
She could be a stepsister,
or an adopted sister.
She is carrying crutches
for the girl in the wheelchair.

The Disney worker
lets the wheelchair girl
and the other blond girls in,
but stops the Asian girl,
and closes the gate.
Disabled and family only, she says.

The Asian girl hands the crutches
to one of the blond girls
and whispers, *Remind her to limp!*

Jake turns and glares at the Asian girl.
She smiles at him, and disappears.
DING-DING-DING! Cheater Alert!
A siren goes off in Jake's head.

DING-DING-DING!
Jake is feeling another brain wiser.

10 / Wheelchair

After the Pirates ride,
Minn's mother remembers,
Doesn't Soup
have to go to the bathroom?

Ziploc bag, Jake says.

Minn winces. *Disgusting!*

Minn decides
that the Haunted Mansion is next.
But before they get in line,
she and her father
will take everyone's tickets
and get Fastpasses
for Indiana Jones.

Jake whispers to Halmoni
and then announces
that while Minn gets the Fastpasses,
he will get a wheelchair.

A wheelchair? Minn asks.

Yes, a wheelchair, Jake says.
Halmoni's feet are hurting
and she can hardly walk,
especially with that heavy purse.

Jake returns
with the wheelchair
at the same time
that Minn returns
with Fastpasses
for Indiana Jones—

for three hours from now.

Jake tells Minn to go ahead
to the Haunted Mansion
with her parents.
We'll just hang out and wait for you.
Call my cell phone when you're done.
Meet back here, OK?

As soon as Minn disappears
around the corner,
Jake springs into action.
He pushes Halmoni in the wheelchair.
Soup climbs onto her lap.
Jake is straining
to maneuver the wheelchair,
and it doesn't help
when a boy on a leash
runs right in front
of Halmoni's rolling wheelchair,
dragging his mother behind him.

Jake pulls back on the wheelchair
with all his strength
to keep from running them over.

Hard day?
The Disney worker
at the disabled gate to Small World
pouts in sympathy.

*It's impossible to get around here
with a wheelchair,* Jake says.
*People just cut you off.
One guy knocked my grandmother's shoe off.
It's so rude!*

Well, welcome to Small World,
the Disney worker says in a soothing voice.
*Everybody feels better after Small World.
There is no such word as 'rude' here.
Can your grandmother walk a little bit?
Can she climb into the boat?*

Soup says, *She can walk—*

But not real well, Jake finishes,
yanking Soup's arm.
It's her diabetes.
He whispers,
She's going to have her foot cut off.

Wait time: 1 minute
Duration of ride: 14 minutes.
A one-minute wait
for 14 minutes of riding bliss,

with air conditioning
and happy music thrown in for free.

Jake feels five brains wiser.
We're not hurting anybody, really,
he says to himself.
The kid on the leash and his mom
and the guy who knocked off the shoe
had to wait a little longer—
but they deserve to wait!

Next they zoom through the wheelchair line
at Indiana Jones
and still have time for Teacups
before Minn calls and says,
*We're almost at the front of the line
in Haunted Mansion—
have you had a chance
to do ANYTHING fun?*

Soup is eager to tell Minn
how he, Jake, and Halmoni walked (or rolled)
straight into Small World
and (the not-too-scary) Indiana Jones.
Teacups didn't have a wheelchair line,
but that line was short and fast.
*Minn! We need to get a wheelchair
for your mom, too—
and you can zoom past everyone,
just like us!*

Minn raises an eyebrow.
Jake, you're a cheater!

But Minn's father pats Jake on the back.
Now that's thinking!
That's a smart boy, Grandma!

It hurts here, and here, and here,
Halmoni says, grabbing her leg.
Pain, such pain!

Minn turns her face away from Jake.
Her eyes are burning.

Jake says,
What about those girls
with the wheelchair
at Pirates of the Caribbean?
Those boys cutting in line,
pretending that their mom
was up ahead.
At every single ride here,
someone is cheating.
Why not me?
At least Halmoni really does
have a walking problem.
So it's not a lie. Not exactly.
'Pain, such pain'; you heard her!

All through lunch
Minn has her Minnster Face on—
serious and unforgiving.

She tears into her pizza,
ripping it apart,
devouring it
like a velociraptor.

Jake slurps his Coke loudly,
to bug her.

You should be drinking milk,
Minn says. *So you can grow.*

Point for Minn.

I HAVE been growing, Jake says.
Just not like an oddball GIRAFFE.

Point for Jake.

And you know what else? Jake adds.
If I looked like an oddball giraffe,
I would stop drinking milk!

2–1. Jake scores again!

But Jake is beginning to wonder:
Who's right here, anyway?
Who's wrong?

Jake decides that Minn is right,
at least about one thing.
Starting tomorrow:
MILK!

11 / Three Little Lizards

SOUP!
A familiar voice
is calling from the churros cart.
Soup! Jake! Over here!

Soup spots Jeremy and Haylee Hirata
standing with their parents
in the churros line.
Misha is there, too.
Soup rushes over to them.
Jeremy, Misha, and Soup jump up
to bump chests.

I have your lizards! Soup whispers.

Here? At Disneyland? Where?
Misha pokes at Soup's pockets.

In their jar, in a paper bag,
in Halmoni's purse—
and she doesn't even know it!

Soup tells Misha and Jeremy
how they rolled past the lines
with Halmoni in the wheelchair.
Haylee can't believe it.
Jake walks up to her and she says,
Is it true? You went straight through
on Indiana Jones?

Jake tells Haylee the story
while Haylee eats a churro.
Sugar on her lips,
she sparkles.

Minn frowns.
Go over and meet Jake's friend,
Minn's mother says.

Wait! Minn's father says.
When do you want to leave
for the California Adventure side?
Your mom wants to do Soarin'—
so we better get going
if we're going to get back
for our Fastpasses for Indiana Jones.
Ready?

Not yet, Minn says.

Her father taps his watch.
Not yet? Then when?

Minn shrugs.
Minn doesn't feel much like riding Soarin'
or any other rides.

Haylee shrieks,
Jake, you're so smart!
Hi, there, long lost Grandma!
[cackle, snort]
Hi, there, Cousin Soup!

Jake leans close to Haylee
and mumbles something.
She smells sweet, he thinks.
Minn walks up
as Haylee purrs at Jake,
Ditch her!
Spend the day with me!

Minn glares.
Jake's ears turn red.
This is Haylee, Jake says.
Pointing to Minn, he says to Haylee,
Um, that's Minn.

Haylee flashes Minn a sparkly smile.
I think I heard about you.
Well, you're definitely—like—TALL!

Minn answers,
Did you hear I catch lizards, too?

At the mention of lizards,
Haylee makes a face.
Whatever, she says.
She looks Minn up and down
and her eyes rest on Minn's dirty fingernails,
then shift to her own
perfectly polished nails,
shining like ten rubies
on the tips of her fingers.

Minn says,
Jake, my mom wants to go
to Soarin'.
Should we leave now?
Are you coming or not?

—

Soup skips back to the table
where Halmoni and Minn's parents
are sitting and drinking coffee.
Soup digs through Halmoni's purse
to get his paper bag.
As Soup dashes back
to Jeremy and Misha,
Minn's father shouts,
Soup, ask Minn WHEN!

So Soup makes a detour,
skipping back to Minn, and asks.
When?

Now, Soup, Minn says. *NOW!*

—

AAACCCKKK! Lizards! EEEEEEEEK!

Jake and Haylee look behind them.
A woman is screaming,
hands on her head.
Misha, Soup, and Jeremy

are darting around
Haylee's legs,
grasping at air.
Haylee looks down
just in time
to see three lizards
running over her feet.

AAAAAAAAAACCCCKKKKKKK!
Haylee hops up on a chair,
screaming.
Get them away!
Get them away from me!

They're only lizards,
three little lizards.
It's nothing!
Jake shouts.

Don't shout at me, Jake!
Haylee shouts.
It's your stupid brother!
It's your stupid brother's fault!

Soup starts to cry.

Minn quickly catches
the three loose lizards
and moves them to the bushes.

Haylee is still trembling
and still standing on the chair.

Minn is tempted
to catch the lizards again
and put them down
Haylee's shirt.

She quickly covers her mouth,
to hide her laughter.

Soup is still crying. He runs up
and tries to hold Jake's hand,
but Jake shakes him off.

Soup, why did you ruin everything?
Jake yells.
Why can't you leave me alone?

Minn shoots a killer look at Jake.
She scoops Soup up in her arms
and gives him a big hug,
then squats down
and holds his head in her hands,
and stares straight into
his teary eyes.

Soup, don't feel bad.
It's not your fault
if some sugar-coated girl
and her cheating boyfriend
can't deal with
three little lizards!

12 / 59 Seconds

Jake wakes up late the next morning,
as usual. 11:57 a.m.
It is almost not morning anymore.
Was that a rough night,
or just a bad dream?

Unusual noises
are coming from the living room.
Jake peeks.
He sees Halmoni
moving stacks of books,
mainly Bibles
of different sizes and colors.
She seems to be searching
for something.

Now Jake remembers:
She is packing for the hospital.
Tomorrow
she will have Roto-Rooter on her leg.

Soup is playing a video game.
Jake sits down on the couch next to Soup.
Soup scoots away and yells,
Why can't you leave me alone?!

Jake goes back to bed.
He is staring up at the ceiling.
His friends, the floaters, return.

He follows them around the room,
and questions drift into his mind.
Jake pulls out his notebook
and writes:

How am I going to make
any trades this summer?
How am I going to make
any money this summer?

Was it really wrong to cut in line
with the wheelchair?
Was it really wrong to yell at Soup?
Why did Soup bring lizards to Disneyland?

Why was Minn so mad at me?
What did I ever do to her?

Slowly, fuzzy memories of his bad deeds
push their way into his mind and, reluctantly,
into his notebook:

1. Not writing Minn a single letter all summer
2. Not calling Minn back when I said I would
3. Not paying attention to Minn
   when Haylee was there

Number 3 was probably the killer.
He decides to call Minn.
She should be in the Reptile House
at the San Diego Zoo about now.

Minn's mother answers.

Hello? Hi, this is Jake. Is Minn there?

Minn is in heaven.
She's been in the Reptile House for an hour.
The place gives me the creeps.
Wait! Here she comes!

Why are you calling? Minn says.

Jake stutters,
I just— just wanted to tell you—
Tell you that— that—
that you were right.

He didn't plan on apologizing, exactly.
But the apologies are tumbling out,
and now it's too late to stop.
You were right about yesterday.
About the wheelchair.
And I shouldn't have snapped at Soup.
I'm glad you hugged him.
Sorry. That's it.
Go see some more animals now—

Minn cannot believe her ears.
What?

Nothing, Jake says.
Just forget it. Go see the animals.

No, you were right, too, Jake!
Your grandmother was really limping
in the parking lot on the way back.
I feel bad because
we weren't paying attention to her
in the beginning.
We should've had a wheelchair
from the start!

They argue like polite chipmunks
about who was wrong
or more wrong,
or most wrong,
or most-often wrong.

Jake tells her to come back
and see the pet store tomorrow,
but Minn's plane leaves first thing
in the morning.

Minn says,
I'm going to do a chess camp.
Next week.
You want to do it with me?

Jake says, *I'll check.*
Check! Like in checkmate. Get it?
He winces.
Why does he say such dumb things?
My mom has to help Halmoni
after her surgery,
but my dad will be in Santa Brunella,

so it might be OK for me
to come back early.

Minn says,
You can stay at my house.
And every day after chess camp
we can catch lizards
and dig tunnels for worms, or—
anything you want!
Hey, can I talk to Soup?

Soup perks up,
hearing Minn's name.

Soup, give your brother
a big hug for me,
OK?
I miss you both already!

Jake looks at his phone:
59 seconds.

All those hours
of being angry
with each other
disappear
with a 59-second talk
on the phone.

Jake grabs his notebook:

59 Seconds
Object of Game:
The world is coming to an end.
You have 59 seconds to change
the course of world history.

I did it, Jake thinks.
I have changed my world:
from the worst summer to . . . who knows?

It might turn out
to be the best summer ever.